The Adventures of Lars and Willow

THE PURFECT ESCAPE

By

Samantha Winters

This book is dedicated to:

To my Dad who was neither a big lover of dogs or cats, but was full of dreams, ideas, and ice cream. He encouraged me to always pursue my passions and taught me that "the only person that can stop you is yourself". May he be forever smiling down on me and our house full of animals.

It's morning and I have learned the routine. Wake up, say hello to my human family members with a wag of the tail and a slobbery kiss all while running at top speed directly into their bodies. No matter the size of the family member - big or small, they all get the same greeting with the same level of enthusiasm and gusto. I loved it.

This was all followed by a big bowl of yummy breakfast of squishy, cold, smelly tuna fish fresh out of this glorious metal container. Bellies and hearts full we rushed to the door to frolic outside.

We would wait patiently, ok well, maybe not so patiently, ahem, Willow, to have our harness put on, leash attached, and we were off. Or at least I thought. Each morning the same routine - tail wag, slobbery kiss, full sprint, delicious food and then....Not so fast Lars! What was the problem? I followed the routine just as my brother Bodie and sister Willow did, but I was never allowed to frolic outside. Oh the frolicking, it looks so magical. There are squirrels to chase, poop to sniff, grass to eat, and freedom to feel the breeze on our face and the wind in our whiskers.

MEOW. MEEEOOOOWWW! As I stand at the full length glass door looking outside, I realize no one can hear me and I am definitely not going outside! I wait and wait and finally Bodie and Willow come back from their adventures, and I so wish they could tell me all about it, but all they can say is WOOOF! As Willow settles into her post-walk nap, I quickly run over and snuggle in tight under her wet slobbery chin. The drips of slobber keep me cool on this hot summer day and the gentle rumbles from her snoring provide a constant comforting tune as we drift into slumber.

In my slumber I started to let my mind drift back to the days when I would snuggle next to my Momma and she would tell me the wisdoms of the world. She wanted to teach me all the life lesson before I headed out of the house forever. You can be anything you want to be Lars you just have to put your mind to it. The only person who can stop you is yourself. Live your dreams, live them big. Create, explore, try, do. Dare to be uniquely you. You will have challenges and setbacks, successes, and celebrations as you explore this life you are given.

As I start to wake up from my nap, I look at Willow and she looks at me. I see her fluffy orange fur and her big white paws. She certainly looks like me. But, I think I am a cat and I think she is a dog. Could I be a dog? I feel like a dog. I can do everything a dog can do – I run, I poop, I give my human family kiss and love. I see no difference. Ok, maybe one difference. She lets out great big WOOFs that nearly knocks anyone off their feet. My MEOW is BARELY heard. A mere squeak.

I wonder to myself...Does it matter? You are a cat, Willow is a dog, but that should not define us. We should not let that stop us, because the only person who can stop you is yourself....and I don't plan to stop!

Full of my new confidence to live the life I want. I start to plot my plan. I must get outside! But how, oh how am I going to do this. Perhaps I could be wheeled outside by one of my human sisters while they play store. Yes, that is it. I will jump in the cart. They will never know!

Perhaps that is not the best plan. I am getting bigger, and my head is towering over this cart. They will certainly see me. Ok, new plan. I will hide under the stool in the mudroom. They will never see me! As soon as the door opens to let Willow and Bodie out for the morning, I will dash from the hiding spot and out the door. Ah, yes, it is a purfect plan.

The next morning we woke up and went through the routine - tail wag, slobbery kiss, full sprint, delicious food and then....Not so fast Lars! NOOOOOO! I have been discovered. I guess my hiding spot was not as secure as I had originally thought. And here I am again, looking out from the inside.

Ok, new plan. I will curl up under Willow's chin and when she gets up to go out the door, I will jump on her back, and we will ride outside together. Willow was particularly skeptical about this plan, but I knew I had to try something. We had the same fur; perhaps no will notice I am there. I will just blend in. No one can find anything in that fur, let alone a small little kitten. The plan was purfect! Until it wasn't....

Ok this is my last hope of getting outside. I must take matters into my own paws and make this happen. There is a small window in the mudroom that is often left open. It has a screen on it, but I think, wait, I know I can knock it off. Then it is just a short jump from there and I will be out!

There was only one small glitch. Bodie! He loved to sit on the path just outside the window. I hoped he would not see me and if he did, he would not say a word. He was at times unreliable....like that time he led Willow into the woods. Well, I am just going to have to take my chances.

And here I go....I pushed and I pushed with all my might and then suddenly, the screen popped off, and out I jumped. I ran down the path and onto the lawn. Oh the lawn! The grass tickled my paws, the wind blew back my fur, and then squish! YUCK! I just stepped in the biggest, smelliest, poop freshly dropped by Willow herself! Thanks girl, my first adventure out of the house and this is how you welcome me.

Once I cleaned myself off, I looked for Willow to show me the way. We ran through the grass, we chased squirrels, and barked at the birds.

We even learned to roll down the hill on our backs thanks to the fine instruction from Bodie. Oh the fun we had, the memories we made, the joy we felt.

Soon it was time to head back home. Willow led the way through the long grass, up the hill, into our warm welcoming home. I filed right in behind Willow as if it was normal operating proceedure. Hoping that my mother and father did not realize what had just occurred.

We ran right in and laid down on the cool hard floor, snuggled close to each other and we both let out roaring giggles thinking about the adventure we just had.

And now time for my nap, and to plan my next adventure....

About the Author:

Samantha Winters moved with her family from New York City to Vermont to follow their dreams of living a simplier life - one filled with joy and giggles. She has 3 daughters who are constantly encouraging her to give into her desire to fill their home with animals. It took over 2 years to convince her husband to say yes to a cat – as he is more of a dog lover. Her oldest daughter's friend happened to have kittens to give away and finally the family could not resist anymore. Immediately when they brought Lars home, they knew it was the right choice. He instantly blended with the family and provides constant amusement to them all. His interactions with the family dogs, especially Willow were so entertaining that Samantha knew that she must share it with all through a children's book.

About Willow Wilhemina Winters:

She is currently 1.5 years old and her most recent weight was 118lbs (she's still growing). She is originally from a farm in Upstate New York. She is one of the sweetest dogs you will ever meet. She is also one of the messiest. You will not escape a meeting with her clean. She will cover you with slobber, hair and love.

About Bodie Duke Winters:

He is currently 5 years old and 110 pounds. He was born and raised in Vermont. He is relentlessly friendly, incredibly handsome but struggles with obedience. He enjoys eating socks, underwear, and scrunchies. Luckily, Bodie usually makes sure they leave his stomach before they take a ride through his intestines.

About Lars Anderson Winters:

He is a tiny kitten who was a born in Vermont. His mother was a barn cat and his father a stray. Despite his tiny size he often initiates rumbles with his dog brother and sister. He has also been known to sleep in their bed, which is neither welcomed nor encouraged.

Made in United States
Orlando, FL
23 August 2022

21481415R00015